I prayed someone would start talking soon. The silence was killing me.

Dad cleared his throat. AHEM! "Tabitha and Jason, I hope you will learn something from this. First of all, if you thought the animal was wild, you should never have picked it up."

Jason interrupted. "We figured it was a miracle."

Daddy looked confused for a minute, then said, "In this case, it wasn't a miracle, and that isn't a wild rabbit. It's probably a pet that got loose."

Jason's father took his glasses off and cleaned them with his handkerchief. "Son, when I told you that you could give the rabbit to Tabitha, I assumed you would ask her parents! I certainly didn't think you'd put it in the cage with Hoppy."

He put his glasses back on and glared at Jason. "Didn't I tell you that two rabbits together ends up to be more rabbits?"

Pickle Stew

A TABITHA SARAH BIGBEE BOOK

BY WENDY LORD

Chariot Books™
David C. Cook Publishing Co.

IT'S A
FLIP
BOOK!

Chariot Books™ is an imprint of David C. Cook Publishing Co.
David C. Cook Publishing Co., Elgin, Illinois 60120
David C. Cook Publishing Co., Weston, Ontario
Nova Distribution Ltd., Newton Abbot, England

PICKLE STEW
© 1994 by Wendy Lord

Designed by Cheryl Blum
Cover illustration by Paul Casale
Internal illustrations by Kate Flanagan
First Printing, 1994
Printed in the United States of America
98 97 96 95 94 5 4 3 2 1

Library of Congress Cataloging-in-Publication Data
Lord, Wendy.
Pickle stew / by Wendy Lord.
p.   cm.
Summary: Tabitha learns that rich next-door neighbor Jason can be
helpful in a crisis, even though he is irresponsible about the babies their
pet rabbits have.
ISBN 0-7814-0886-5
[1. Rabbits—Fiction. 2. Family life—Fiction. 3. Friendship—Fiction. 4.
Christian life—Fiction.] I. Title.
PZ7.L8785Pi   1994
[Fic]—dc20   93-19018
                                                        CIP
                                                        AC

To the real Tabitha Sarah Bigbee who so
graciously agreed to let me use her name for
this book, and then has practically grown up,
waiting for me to finish it.

WL

"I have told you these things, so that in me
you may have peace. In this world you will
have trouble. But take heart!
I have overcome the world."

John 16:33

Contents

·1·

Soup Starter

My name is Tabitha Sarah Bigbee, and I've had more pickle stew than most kids get in a lifetime. Actually, only half of it was rightfully mine. The rest belonged to Jason Harrington. My grammy says, "The difference between pickle stew and just plain old trouble, is that pickle stew is trouble that's not really your fault."

I can tell you for sure that those nine rabbits were not my fault!

I don't suppose they were Jason's fault, either. But trouble is trouble, and it sure would have been nice to have some help from Jason, or at least some sympathy.

Jason's rabbit was the father and my

rabbit was the mother, and I was stuck buying rabbit feed forever, because Jason Harrington is totally irresponsible.

Like I said, those nine rabbits were not my fault. But I might as well explain right from the beginning how all this rabbit trouble got started.

There's a potato field between Jason's house and my house. After school one day last spring, we were playing down by the edge of the woods that runs along behind the field. Jason was supposed to be counting, because it was my turn to hide.

I heard, "Ten, twenty, thirty, for . . . Hey, Tabitha, come here! Look at this rabbit!"

"You're not supposed to look at anything, Jason," I yelled. "Count with your eyes shut."

"Come here!" he hollered again. "You won't believe it!"

It was a gorgeous red rabbit. I thought all rabbits were either plain brown or

10

ordinary white like Jason's rabbit, Hoppy. But this rabbit was like nothing I had ever seen. Its fur was a silky reddish orange, just the color of my Aunt Connie's hair.

"I wish we could catch him," I told Jason.

I no sooner said that than the rabbit looked up and hopped directly over to us! Jason was used to handling rabbits, so he thought he'd try to pick it up.

No problem. The rabbit practically leapt into his arms!

"See, Tabitha," he said, "we wished we could catch him, and we did. Our wish came true."

"Oh, Jason. Wishes don't just come true all by themselves! It's a miracle, that's what. God gave me a miracle."

But Jason didn't think much of that. "God didn't give you a miracle, Tabitha. It's me who's got the rabbit."

Now about here we got into sort of a fight, but Jason did know more about rabbits, and we were closer to his house. The silky red

11

rabbit was getting a little nervous with all the fighting, so I gave in, and we took the rabbit to Jason's house.

His father saw us coming, opened the kitchen door, and said one word. "No."

Of course Jason asked why not, and his father said, "Because you already have a rabbit. Two rabbits turns into too many rabbits!"

"Can I give it to Tabitha?"

"Sure," his father said. "That would suit me just fine." Then he slammed the kitchen door.

We started home with my beautiful rabbit.

"Tabitha, why don't you name him Red?" suggested Jason.

Jason would call him Red. He has absolutely no imagination. Our dog's name is Everett, but Jason insists on calling him Blacky.

He used to call me Tabby, which I absolutely hate. It almost broke up our friendship. But there aren't many kids on our road, and I need someone to hang around with. So I had Grammy speak to him.

"Young man," she said with this ferocious scowl on her face, "I'm asking you to respect Tabitha's wishes and call her by her proper name. Around this house we respect each other! Is that clear?"

Apparently it was, because he mumbled, "Yes, ma'am," and never called me Tabby again.

I wanted my rabbit to have a real classy name like Churchill or Androcles or Abraham. By the time we got almost to my house I had settled on Androcles, but I suddenly realized that I didn't have a cage for him.

Jason had a great idea. "Hoppy could let old Red stay with him. There's plenty of room in his hutch, and besides, then Hoppy wouldn't be lonely."

When I look back on it now, I realize we should have stopped to think about what Jason's father had said. I know now

13

that the problem with rabbits isn't so much who owns them, but what other rabbits they hang around with.

We didn't think, but we didn't disobey, either. Jason wasn't keeping the rabbit. Androcles was my rabbit, and Jason was just letting him stay overnight.

So we went to Jason's house and put Androcles in Hoppy's cage.

14

Just then Jason's mother called him in for supper, so I shut the garage door and went home. Hoppy had a friend, and Androcles had a warm place to spend the night.

Now that sounds like the happy ending to a nice little story. But it's really only the beginning of pickle stew.

15

2

Add Trouble and Mix Well!

During supper I watched for just the right moment to mention Androcles. Grammy told about the lady who had come to try on the wedding gown Mom was sewing. Mom said the lady spilled coffee on her sewing machine and ruined a whole yard of lace.

Then Dad told us about a family of moose he saw on his milk route that morning.

"That's what I like best about driving the tanker," he said. "I pass long sections of woods and fields between each farm, and there's almost always some sort of wild creature out and about that early in the morning. Once I get the milk back to the dairy, my day becomes a little more

16

ordinary. But those first few hours are really pleasant."

Here was my opening.

"Well, Dad, I saw a wild creature today that I bet you've never seen from your milk truck."

Immediately I had him. About the only thing Dad likes better than wildlife is supper, and right now he was enjoying both.

"Oh?" He mumbled with his mouth full.

"Jason and I saw a huge, silky red rabbit at the edge of the woods today."

"A redheaded rabbit, huh?"

"Yep. It was exactly the color of Aunt Connie's hair."

Dad laughed. "You always have imagined that your hair was the same color as Aunt Connie's. Now you've imagined a rabbit. Well, sweetie, I'm afraid you and the rabbit both have brown hair."

"No, Dad, really. Just ask Jason."

Dad sat back in his chair and laid his fork down firmly beside his plate. "Well,

I guess that confirms it then. Jason Harrington is a most reliable source of information who must not be questioned. Let's remember it was Jason who first informed us of the dinosaurs in the potato house, and the man-eating lizards that planned to take over the Stop 'N' Shop."

"Oh, Daddy, he was only little then!"

Bringing up the subject of Jason was not always a good idea at the supper table, but tonight it could work to my advantage since Dad was having such a good joke over the whole thing.

And then, without even knowing it, Mom supplied the final touch. "You know, I saw these huge red rabbits at the fair once. I'll bet they weighed fifteen pounds. They were called red silks or red something . . . red satins I think."

Dad was not ready to give it up. "Well, if we've got fifteen-pound red rabbits running around in the woods, no wonder there are dinosaurs in the potato house!"

The joke made absolutely no sense at all, but Dad was laughing so hard he was crying.

I didn't plan on saying any more about Androcles yet. It was better to let them just get used to the idea of him first, before they thought about me keeping him.

Later, Grammy and I did the dishes together like we always do. I don't exactly like doing dishes, but I do love this time with Grammy. "Your turn to wash, Gram. I'll go wipe the table."

Grammy was running water into the sink when I came back. Without turning around, she said, "So, tell me about your rabbit."

Finally, a sympathetic listener. I told her all about how we found him and how he was so friendly and how Jason's father said he couldn't keep him.

I took a deep breath. "So, I thought I'd ask Dad and Mom if I could keep him."

Grammy dried her hands and turned to face me. "Where's the rabbit now, Tabitha?"

The next few hours were kind of confusing. After a discussion with Grammy, I called Jason. Then his dad called my dad. Then my dad called the veterinarian. The next thing we knew Jason and I were sitting with rabbits in boxes on our laps in the vet's waiting room.

Later, back at home, I sat staring at the circle of feet around my living room. Mom's and Daddy's feet were across from me in front of the sofa. Jason's feet were right beside me, swinging back and forth under the piano bench. Mr. and Mrs. Harringtons' feet shuffled in front of the love seat. In the kitchen, Everett was right underneath Grammy's feet as usual.

I prayed someone would start talking soon. The silence was killing me.

Dad cleared his throat. AHEM! "Tabitha and Jason, I hope you will learn something from this. First of all, if you thought the ani-

mal was wild, you should never have picked it up. The vet told us there's a rabies epidemic this year. Rabies is a deadly disease that you can get from sick animals. If an animal has rabies, it may not act afraid of you like it naturally would. So, if any animal ever comes up to you, leave it alone and come home."

Jason interrupted. "We figured it was a miracle."

21

Daddy looked confused for a minute, then said, "In this case, it wasn't a miracle, and that isn't a wild rabbit. The vet said it's a red satin, a kind of rabbit that's raised for show. But since it has no registration number tattooed in its ear, it's probably a pet that got loose.

"Hoppy's ear was torn pretty badly," Daddy went on, "but Dr. Jonas stitched it, so it will heal nicely. The red rabbit is only missing some fur."

Jason's father took off his glasses and cleaned them with his handkerchief. "Son, when I told you that you could give the rabbit to Tabitha, I assumed you would ask her parents! I certainly didn't think you'd put it in the cage with Hoppy."

He put his glasses back on and glared at Jason. "Didn't I tell you that two rabbits together ends up to be more rabbits?"

I figured I'd better jump in here. It was starting to sound like we did it on purpose. "But Androcles was just visiting until I

22

could ask about him and get a cage at our house. We didn't know they would fight. Anyway, we didn't think it would hurt to have two boy rabbits in the same hutch."

Daddy cleared his throat. "Actually, that's the biggest problem. Androcles is not a boy, and Dr. Jonas seems to think she's going to have babies. If we can't find the owner, we're going to have a lot of bunnies around here in about a month. You'll have to find homes for them."

All this time, I sat and stared at the floor mostly. Every now and then, I glanced toward the kitchen hoping that Grammy would give me a glimmer of hope, but she wouldn't look at me. Grammy was my very best friend, but when I was in trouble with Mom or Dad, she stayed out of it.

"I know you two really didn't mean for this to happen," Dad said.

I breathed a sigh of relief, because it sounded like they were going to let us off the hook. But the lecture continued.

"When you put an animal into another animal's territory, they usually fight, even gentle animals like rabbits. That hutch was Hoppy's private space, his safe place. And he defended it, even if he did get to like Androcles for a mate."

I guess Jason and I were looking pretty miserable by then, because suddenly Daddy smiled and his shoulders slumped. "I've got some boards and chicken wire. If you can't find the owner, I'll build a cage for Androcles in the chicken yard."

I jumped up and hugged him. "Oh, thank you, Daddy!"

Jason just sat there.

"Meanwhile," Daddy went on, "I've put a chicken crate on the back porch. The rabbit must stay in there at night. You can let him, I mean her, out to run on the porch to get some exercise during the day. Just clean up after her and remember to push something in front of the screen door.

"That door won't stay shut anymore," he

24

explained to the Harringtons. "The support posts are rotting away underneath and the end is sagging. The handrail is loose, and I don't think those steps are safe anymore. If I don't rebuild that porch soon, it'll just keep leaning down the hill until it ends up in the potato field!"

The adults laughed and started talking about old houses and how hard it is to get around to doing repairs.

I couldn't imagine Mr. Harrington doing repairs.

They live in a brand-new, one-story house. He's a lawyer, and Mrs. Harrington is a nurse. I don't think lawyers and nurses tear down old porches.

All of a sudden the grown-ups remembered why they were there, and Jason and I were the center of attention again.

Mom nudged Daddy and reminded him about the twenty-four dollar vet bill.

"Oh, yes," he said. "We think it would be fair for you two to split the vet bill. It's your responsibility, not ours. As Grammy would say, 'This is your pot of pickle stew!'"

"Jason should have to pay for half the bag of rabbit feed too," I said.

Mrs. Harrington quickly jumped into the conversation. "But that would make the rabbit half Jason's. We already told him he couldn't have another pet."

"That's right," Mr. Harrington agreed. "Maybe you'll find the real owner, but otherwise, the rabbit is yours, not Jason's."

All in all, my situation looked pretty hopeless. I hadn't ordered the batch of pickle stew. I hadn't done anything wrong. But I owed twelve dollars for my half of the vet bill and eight dollars for a bag of feed.

"I'll tell you what, though," Jason's father said. "Since Hoppy is going to be the father of the baby bunnies, it's only fair that Jason help you find homes for them when they are born. After all, a father has to live up to his responsibilities too."

The adults laughed, stood up, and shook

26

hands, proud of themselves for solving this mess so neatly. But they didn't know Jason like I did. I knew I'd be left to buy feed for millions of rabbits for the rest of my life!

3

Simmer Slowly

When I say my prayers at night, I always talk to God first about Jason, and then I explain how much I need a Silver Streak skateboard like the one in the picture in my nightstand. Then I thank Him for everyone in my family, especially Grammy.

"All this rabbit business could help you and Jason learn to get along together," Grammy told me.

"I doubt it, Gram. I've been praying for weeks for God to make Jason act right. But either God's not listening to me, or Jason's not listening to God!"

"Tabitha, honey, it doesn't work that way. God doesn't make people act right.

28

They choose how to act."

"If that's the way it is, the whole world must be absolutely drowning in pickle stew. But I'm going to pray about Jason anyway."

I decided I had to talk to God about Androcles, too, because even though she was expensive, I wanted to keep her. But I truly did try to find the real owner.

Every day after school, if Mom or Daddy went somewhere in the car, I went along. We stopped at all the neighbors' houses to ask if anyone had lost a rabbit. No one had. But when we were at the Kreiders' house, which is on the other side of the woods behind us, we found a clue.

"The house next to ours has been empty for about a week," Mrs. Kreider said. "I think the family who moved out of there came from Texas. They only stayed a few months. I don't know if they had a rabbit. They did have a bunch of dogs and cats, though. Why don't you call the real estate agent and try to get hold of them?"

29

On the lawn outside that house was a sign that said Windham Realty. I wrote down the number.

When we got home it took me about an hour to get up the nerve to call. I hate calling people I don't know! The phone hardly finished ringing once, when suddenly there was a fuzzy recorded voice telling me to leave a message. I hung up.

Grammy called the next morning and explained what we wanted. She found out that the house belonged to the Northeast National Bank.

"The family who moved out of that house rented it from us," the bank lady said. "And I think they moved back to Texas. Or was it Tennessee? In any case, I don't have their address. I'm sorry."

I was sorry too. But not real sorry. It looked more and more like I was going to get to keep Androcles.

The next day Grammy stopped the mailman and asked if he knew where

30

the Kreiders' neighbors had moved.

"No, ma'am, Mrs. Bigbee," he said. "They didn't leave a forwarding address. I've been marking all their mail 'Return to Sender.'"

When I got home from school, Grammy filled me in.

"Tabitha," she said, "we can't go chasing down everyone in Texas and Tennessee to find out if they used to own a red rabbit! As I see it, the only thing left to do is ask your daddy to build a hutch in the chicken yard. Looks like you got yourself a rabbit."

That was exactly what I'd been praying for every single night since I found Androcles.

We discussed the rabbit situation at supper that night.

"I've been thinking this over," Daddy said. "I could build the hutch into the side of the chicken house with a separate door to the outside. That way it would stay warmer at night, and it wouldn't be so hard to build."

Daddy grabbed his paper napkin and

made a little drawing. "See, there could be a sliding tray here to clean it out, and I could put a sheet of insulation under the tray."

"That would make things easier for Tabitha," Grammy said. "She has to go in the yard to let the chickens out every day anyway."

"Daddy," I asked, "do you think when I let Androcles out to play, the chickens will hurt her?"

"I don't think so," he said. "She's bigger than most of the hens, and she can run faster. Just watch her and let me know if there's a problem."

So Daddy built a hutch. From inside the chicken house, the rabbit hutch looked just like a little box in the corner. I don't think the chickens cared that there was a rabbit in there. But they liked to sit on the hutch at night and peek in at her through the wire vents on each side.

I was worried about keeping her outside throughout the winter. Winters in northern Maine are very cold. But I read in the encyclopedia that rabbits can live in extremely cold weather as long as they are dry and out of the drafts. So the chicken coop would do fine.

Androcles was a great pet. I let her out in the chicken yard every day for some exercise. At first the chickens were afraid of her. Every time she made a move, they'd scatter in a flurry of dust.

"Chickens are such big babies, aren't they, Grammy? They're suspicious of everything. And they aren't very smart."

"You're right about that," she answered. "When the sun starts going down, you'd think they would know to get inside the chicken house for the night, and most of them do. But there are always a few that fool around too long and suddenly realize it's getting dark."

"Yeah," I said, "and instead of just going inside, they sit in a heap under the ramp and worry. Then I've got to chase them around the yard and get them in. I think they do it on purpose for a little excitement."

In the morning I open the chickens' door, and most of them come out in a huge flurry. Then the stragglers come parading down the ramp like they are in some kind of a fashion show.

One morning last summer, Grammy went out to feed them, and just as she opened the gate, a branch fell out of the maple tree and landed in their yard. You would think they'd be used to that. Branches and sticks are always falling out of that tree because it's mostly dead. But everything is such a big deal to chickens.

When the branch hit the ground, they scrambled in a panic out the gate. My dog, Everett, chased them across the road to Mr. Jepson's house. The dog and thirty-two hens played a grand game of tag with Mr. Jepson, back and forth across his petunias. It was quite a spectacle, with yelling and squawking and barking and dirt flying everywhere.

34

Everett finally gave up and hid under our front porch. But the chickens stayed and had breakfast in Mr. Jepson's vegetable garden.

"You can't blame them for that," Grammy sighed.

We feed them vegetable scraps, and they're especially fond of peas and strawberries, which Mr. Jepson has a lot of . . . or used to.

35

Mr. Jepson came across the road to talk to Grammy. Well, he didn't actually come across. He sort of stormed across, and talking isn't exactly the right word either.

Grammy put her apron over her head, and muttered, "I believe this is the most awful pot of pickle stew I've had all year."

She was probably right, because Mr. Jepson, who is actually Grammy's friend and who comes for dinner on Sundays, said some rude things, like he wished a logging truck had come along while all the animals were crossing the road.

But he came for dinner the next Sunday as usual. Grammy served him peas and strawberries and chicken. Mr. Jepson and Grammy and I laughed about that until we could hardly swallow, but I don't think Mom and Dad got the joke.

Eventually the chickens got used to Androcles. If they touched her, she'd kick her hind legs and leap out of the way.

36

They got tired of that and mostly ignored her.

In a few weeks Androcles's tummy was getting really big because of her babies. I didn't pick her up. She was so heavy I was afraid I would drop her or hold her too tight. So Daddy and I built a ramp to the door of her hutch so she could get back in herself. I'd let her out to play for a while after school, and then she'd climb right back in when she saw me getting her feed ready.

Just before the babies were due to be born, Androcles didn't want to go out at all, and the bag of feed that we'd bought in the beginning was almost gone. I didn't have any money, and my piggy bank had coughed up only enough to pay off the first three dollars of my debt. I still owed seventeen dollars and had no idea at all how I was going to get it.

I decided to go see Jason.

37

•4•

··

Hot Pepper in the Pot

I found Jason on his back step reading a
skateboard magazine. I told him how we
had searched for Androcles's owner and how
Dad had made a hutch. I was hoping to
impress him with the fact that our family
had done a lot of work and he hadn't done
any. Androcles was my rabbit, but the
babies were half his.

He didn't get the point.

"Androcles has been eating an awful lot,"
I told him. "She needs extra food because
her babies are due soon. The bag of feed is
almost gone."

He still didn't get the point.

"Look, Jason, this stew we're in is as

much your fault as mine. You get a lot of allowance, and I don't get any. I still have seventeen dollars to pay. I think you should buy the next bag of feed. You can afford it."

Jason didn't think so at all. "Tabitha, I'm saving to buy a skateboard and I've almost got enough. I paid my half of the vet bill, and that set me back almost two weeks. Why don't you get your mom to buy the feed?"

I knew then and there I was beat. Jason didn't understand how it was at my house. He always has plenty of cash. He has to take out the trash and feed Hoppy, but mostly he does whatever he wants. He never has to help out like I do.

I left Jason with his nose buried in his skateboard magazine and wandered back up the road to my house, wondering how I could get a job.

In our family, only my dad has a real job. The rest of us have to do what we call "pulling our own weight." That means everyone has to help out somehow, so there's not too much load on any one person.

Grammy keeps the chickens and sells most of the eggs to the neighbors. She uses just about every inch of our backyard for a garden, and whatever we don't eat, she cans or freezes for winter. She also makes jam and pickles. "Stocking up," as Grammy calls it, is pretty much a full-time job for her.

Mom sews clothes for people, mostly wedding gowns or prom dresses.

Dad will pull the newspaper from under a pile of blue satin and say something like, "Marilyn, have you taken on more work than you can handle?"

And Mom will say, "Richard, I'm getting paid $200 to make these dresses." That impresses him and he says, "Well, I guess that's worth looking at the back of your head for the rest of the week."

My job is to help Mom and Grammy, but the best way for me to help is to not ask for

40

things like skateboards and allowance. And rabbit feed.

I headed for the kitchen to talk this over with Grammy. She's the expert on pickle stew.

Just as I hoped, Grammy came through. "Mr. Jepson is due to have a supply of firewood delivered this week. Why don't you go see if he needs someone to help him stack it in the shed?"

Mr. Jepson said he could pay me ten dollars for a day's slavery, and I agreed.

When I saw my dad's car pull into our driveway, I said good-bye to Mr. Jepson. "See you Saturday," he called after me.

I found Daddy inspecting the back steps that lead up to the closed-in porch. The dog was bouncing around and acting foolish like he always does when Daddy comes home.

"Well, Everett, my man," Daddy was saying, "what do you think? Is this railing going to last the summer or not?"

41

"Hi, Daddy. Guess what!" I announced. "Mr. Jepson hired me to help him stack firewood."

"So," he said without looking up, "you've decided to be a lumberjack, have you? I really had my heart set on you growing up to be a prizefighter."

"Oh, Daddy. I'm not going to make a career out of it. I just need to earn some money."

He turned and looked at me. "Androcles is getting to be quite a burden, isn't she?"

"Well," I said, "it won't always be this bad. Once her babies are gone, it won't cost so much for food."

Daddy got a very serious look on his face. "Yeah. That's what I keep telling your mother, but she insists on keeping you."

He started to laugh, and I looked around for something to throw at him, but at our house only pillows are legal for throwing when somebody teases you.

He went into the porch and hung up his

42

jacket. Then he sat on the bench, took off his muddy work boots, and reached for his slippers. "I'd like to tear this porch right off the house," he told me. "But then where would I put my boots? I'd have both my mother and my wife ready to thrash me for dragging manure from every farm in the county right into their kitchen. Not a pleasant thought!"

"Daddy, do you like to fix stuff and build things?" I asked him.

"Well, I suppose I do," he answered. "Mostly I just do it around here because I can't afford to hire someone else to do it."

"You mean like the Harringtons do?"

Daddy straightened up and stretched his back. "Now that's a good example. Mr. Harrington would probably hire a construction company to tear off this porch and build a new one. But he does mow his own lawn and clear the snow off his own driveway.

"Time is money, you know. What you don't have money to pay for, you have to do

43

yourself. And what you can't do or don't have time to do yourself, you have to hire someone else to do, like Mr. Jepson hired you."

"Come on," I said, "I want to tell Mom and Grammy about my job. Let's go eat."

After supper, I sat in my room staring at my picture of the Silver Streak skateboard that I would never own. Maybe I should

44

just throw it out. I could ask for a Silver Streak for Christmas, but that was half a year away, and it would be another half a year until the snow disappeared and I could use it.

This summer I'd spend my time working to support a family of rabbits that I didn't ask for. What a life.

Before I went to sleep, I thanked God for my firewood job and asked Him to please do something about Jason.

All week I kept looking for evidence that God had been working on Jason. "Maybe he'll walk up the hill with a bag of Rabbit Chow under his arm," I told Mom.

"And maybe the chickens will scratch up buried treasure under the maple tree," Mom said, pinning the sleeve of a beautiful white gown.

I love watching her work on wedding dresses. I fingered a little piece of white

45

lace. "You just don't have any faith," I said.

"Oh, I have plenty of faith in God. It's Jason I doubt. If I were you, I'd stop expecting the impossible. But I suppose it's okay to hope. Here. Why don't you cut some more squares out of these scraps?"

Mom always gives me the leftover satin. When I have enough squares, I'm going to make a patchwork comforter for my bed. So far I've got white and different shades of blue, but I can never seem to get started sewing them together. I don't think I've inherited my mother's sewing ability. Maybe I should be a lumberjack when I grow up.

Saturday morning I was still asleep, dreaming about a skateboard made out of blue satin patches, when I heard that loud beeping noise a big truck makes when it's backing up. I stuffed my head under my pillow and tried to finish my dream.

Then a roaring, thundering crash brought me out of bed. I got to the window in time to see the truck pull away from a firewood mountain in Mr. Jepson's driveway. The driver was smiling and waving to Mr. Jepson, completely unaware that he had just delivered the most agonizing ten dollars I would ever earn.

Nine More Ingredients?

I think God, or probably Grammy, had been talking to Mr. Jepson, because after I struggled and sweated with his firewood for a whole day, Mr. Jepson gave me ten dollars and a bag of rabbit feed!

I hugged him. "Oh, thank you. Thank you. Thank you. Thank you."

He just grumbled, "I was awful glad to have your help, missy. I'm getting too old for this kind of work."

The next day Mr. Jepson wasn't at church, and he didn't show up for dinner. Grammy and I rushed over to see if he were all right. We found him on the sofa with the heating pad on his shoulders.

"Well, well, neighbor," Grammy said. "I see you've been trying to work like a youngster!"

Mr. Jepson groaned, "The next time I get a load of firewood, I'm going to supervise Tabitha from a lawn chair. Or maybe I'll put in an oil furnace like you folks have."

I felt sorry for Mr. Jepson, but I hoped he didn't get any more firewood for a long time.

My debt was down to seven dollars, and I had a new bag of rabbit feed. But by the looks of Androcles, my situation was going to get worse. She spent most of her day in the hutch, even when I wanted her to come out.

The encyclopedia showed us how to make a nesting box for her to have her babies in. It was a bare wooden box, just big enough for Androcles to get in, with a tall enough edge so the new babies couldn't get out.

We set it inside the hutch, and

49

Androcles loved it. We had given her some dry straw to make a bed in the box. She rearranged it about forty times and then finally threw it out altogether. Then she started pulling out her fur to make a little nest for the babies, just the way the encyclopedia said she would.

On the first day of summer vacation, Androcles became the proud mother of nine little bunnies. And Jason Harrington became the proud owner of a brand-new skateboard.

Jason swung around the end of the railing, leapt up the steps, and burst onto our back porch banging the screen door as he went through. "Tabitha, look what I got!"

"Take it easy on that railing, Jason," Mom called from the house. "Tabitha's outside."

I had been out in the chicken yard admiring Androcles and her new family. I came up into the porch, and there stood Jason with the most magnificent skateboard I had ever seen. It was blue with silver sparkles and had a shiny silver streak that curved and faded away to make it look like it was going fast, even when it wasn't moving at all.

Jason didn't know it, but that was the very skateboard in the picture I kept in my nightstand.

It was hard enough, knowing I would

51

never own a skateboard like that. But now that Jason had one, it was painful.

I changed the subject. "Jason, you're a grandfather!"

"Huh?"

"Androcles had her babies this morning."

"Hey neat! Can I see them?" He started for the hutch.

"Not yet, Jason. We have to leave them alone for a couple days."

When Jason did finally get to see them he thought they were disgusting. "What's the matter with them? They hardly have any hair!"

"They're born without fur, Jason, but they're getting some. And I think they're sweet!"

Some were mostly white with big splotches of red, and some were mostly red with patches of white. But there was one really interesting bunny that was all red with a white ring around his neck. Or her neck.

"I'm going to keep this red one," I told Jason. "When she gets her fur, she'll be gorgeous. But the rest WE will have to find homes for." I put a lot of extra emphasis on the "we," but he didn't seem to notice.

"Just ask around when school starts," Jason said. "I'll bet lots of kids would like to have rabbits. Well, I gotta go. Oh, guess what. My dad said since I was responsible and saved all the money for my skateboard, he's going to build a ramp for me in the backyard!"

My mouth dropped open. "A skateboard ramp?"

"Yep," crowed Jason. "We found the plans for how to build a ramp in my skateboard magazine. Dad says he can have it done for less than $800. He's going to have them put it back where the vegetable garden used to be. The only rotten part is that Dad will have to move some of his precious rosebushes, and he won't do that till they're done blooming. I'll have to wait practically all summer!"

53

Jason took off down the hill on his Silver Streak. I took off for the kitchen to find Grammy. Not only did Jason get my dream skateboard and a ramp, but to top it off, his family thought that a skateboard ramp was a better use for a backyard than a garden! I needed Grammy bad.

I slammed myself into a kitchen chair. Grammy slid an envelope under my nose. I opened it very slowly. I never get any mail. Maybe this was from the people who used to own Androcles. It would be just my luck that they wanted me to pay them for her!

Inside the envelope was a beautiful card and five one-dollar bills!

It was from my other grandmother in Florida, my mom's mother. She always sends me money at the end of the school year. She says it's for my good report card, even though she has long ago stopped asking me to send it to her for proof.

"Grammy," I wailed, "I'm not spending Nana's report card money on rabbit food!"

I ran up to my room.

I decided to put one dollar in the missionary bank at church. We're saving to buy a motorcycle helmet for a nurse in West Africa. She rides between villages on a motor scooter.

The rest I put in my nightstand with my picture of the Silver Streak skateboard. I sealed the envelope and wrote on the outside, "NOT FOR RABBITS." Mom peeked her head in around my door. "I saw that you got a letter today. Was it from Nana?"

I nodded. "She sent me five dollars for my report card. I'm saving most of it right in here for a very special reason." I showed her my envelope.

"Would that special reason happen to be a skateboard?" she asked.

"How did you know?"

"I saw your face when Jason showed you his. And I happen to know you pretty well, Tabitha."

Mom hugged me and I put the

envelope back in my nightstand. No matter how hard I had to work, those rabbits were not getting my report card money!

The rest of my debt and any more feed would have to come from somewhere else.

·6·

Filled to the Brim

It's amazing how fast those bunnies grew! Before long I couldn't hold them with one hand anymore. It's a good thing Daddy made a large hutch, because if they were all going to grow as big as their mother, they were going to be cramped for space.

I took Androcles out for exercise in the chicken yard every day, but I didn't dare let the babies out yet. They weren't big enough to defend themselves against the chickens, and they could have slipped right through the fence.

Everett wasn't allowed in the chicken yard, but he would circle the fence and whine and sniff, especially when Androcles was out. I didn't know if he would hurt the bunnies, but he acted like he'd love to eat one. He was always dragging disgusting-looking dead things out of the woods, real proud like he was some great hunter. I love Everett, but I wasn't letting him near my bunnies.

I named the one with the white ring Pat so it could be a girl's or boy's name, if I ever found out for sure which it was. Grammy came out to feed the chickens, and I asked her to take a look for me.

"I'm not sure, Tabitha. It's pretty hard to tell when they're little, but I think Pat is a girl."

So Pat immediately became Patricia. That is a much more elegant name for such a gorgeous rabbit.

Patricia was the only one I wanted to keep, so I put a sign out front along the road that said, "Baby Rabbits FOR SALE $3.00."

58

From the encyclopedia, I figured I couldn't sell them until sometime in August. They needed to be with their mother for a while. But because our road doesn't go anywhere except into the woods, I figured it wouldn't hurt to advertise early. Probably no one would see the sign except maybe a couple of crusty old French-Canadian loggers, and the ladies

59

who come to try on the dresses that Mom sews.

The summer went by faster than any I could remember, and by August I was still feeding a total of ten very large and very hungry rabbits. I don't think they minded being crowded. In fact, they didn't even use all the space they had. Instead, they piled themselves up in a heap, so that all I could see was a wad of red and white fur with an ear sticking up here and there.

Every few days I'd put a couple rabbits in a box, and Mom and I would go to some of the houses around where we live and try to get rid of one. I'd always say, "The regular price is three dollars but today they're free."

Almost always a kid would say. "Oh, Mom, pleeeese? Isn't it sweet?"

And the mother would say, "But where will we put it?" or "Who's going to take

60

care of it?" or "It'll fight with the cat." The mother always won, and I'd go home with just as many rabbits as before.

I wanted to keep Androcles and Patricia, but that left eight to get rid of. I felt like taking them all over and putting them in Jason's garage. Just once, I'd like him to have to eat pickle stew.

But instead of pickle stew, Mr. Responsible was getting a skateboard ramp. It would serve him right to have to spend some of his precious allowance on rabbit food. I wonder what he's saving for now? A motorcycle probably, or maybe a swimming pool.

It was absolutely not fair, that I, who was responsible, who got no allowance, and who worked like a fool for Mr. Jepson to try to pay off my debt, was still stuck with eight lousy rabbits and a bill for seven dollars.

The bunnies each ate almost as much as Androcles did now. I explained this to Daddy one night at supper, trying to

61

sound very responsibly worried about my problems.

"Look, I know Androcles is mine and I should feed her. But all those babies are half Jason's. They're getting so big, and they eat so much. I've talked to Jason a hundred times about helping me find homes for them. But he won't.

"They're eating a ton of food. He could at least help feed them if he can't get rid of them. He gets a lot of allowance."

Daddy said, "You know, Tabitha, we may never be able to change Jason's attitude. But I'll talk to him for you."

That evening I watched Daddy walk toward the Harringtons' house, praying that God would do another miracle and make Jason take responsibility.

But a little while later, Daddy came home looking embarrassed. I met him at the door.

"Mr. Harrington said Jason is very involved with skateboarding lately and doesn't have time for much else," Daddy said. "Jason said he'd 'ask around when school starts.'"

"I don't suppose Jason gave you any of his precious allowance."

"No, but Mr. Harrington gave me a ten-dollar bill 'to help the kid out some.'"

Daddy gave me the ten dollars. Now I could buy a bag of rabbit food and take another two dollars off my debt.

I know I should have been happy about the ten dollars, but somehow knowing it came from Mr. Harrington instead of Jason made me mad.

I decided to talk to Daddy about getting an allowance, but it made more sense to talk to God first. Then when I talked to Daddy, I might get a miracle.

After a week straight of asking God for an allowance, I decided I was ready to ask my dad. But I didn't come right out and

63

ask, "Can I have an allowance?" No way. During that week of praying, I had also been doing a lot of thinking, and I figured out a strategy.

First I waited until Dad had eaten supper and sat down in the living room. The newspaper was usually on the coffee table, but that afternoon I had put it on the floor beside the sofa. It wasn't really hidden, but it wasn't really in plain view either. It looked like someone had been reading it and laid it there.

I was ready for him.

Daddy put on his reading glasses. "Tabitha, honey, have you seen the newspaper?"

This was going even better than I had hoped, because he called me Tabitha, honey!

"Here it is, Dad." I held out the paper and said, "Daddy, before you read it, can we talk about something?"

He put his glasses back in his pocket.

64

"Sure, honey. What's up?"

Over my shoulder I heard the sewing machine stop. I figured Mom was listening. Good. Maybe I could get her on my side in case I needed some backup support.

"Do you think I pull my weight around here?" I asked.

Daddy looked surprised! "Of course. Why do you ask?"

"Well, I was just wondering if I was a burden to you."

Daddy held me by the shoulders like he always does when he's going to say something he doesn't want me to miss.

"Tabitha Sarah Bigbee. You could never be a burden to me, even if you couldn't do any work at all. If you were weak or even paralyzed it would mean extra work for the rest of us, but you wouldn't be a burden.

"We ask you to pull your weight because you can. Our job is to help you grow into a responsible adult someday. We love you too much to let you grow up spoiled and lazy."

65

Now that was quite a speech for Daddy. I almost forgot about allowance, but I did start thinking about spoiled and lazy. The name Jason Harrington came to mind immediately.

·7·

With Onions

I decided to use Jason to get to the point of this whole conversation: allowance.

"Daddy, do you think the Harringtons should give Jason an allowance if he doesn't pull his weight?"

Daddy thought a minute. "Tabitha, getting an allowance isn't wrong. I'm sure Jason has responsibilities at his house."

"Oh, Daddy. He hardly has to do a thing. And he gets anything he wants. He's even getting a skateboard ramp built right in his own backyard."

"What the Harringtons have or how they raise their son is not our business. Every family has a different arrangement about

67

chores and allowances. Most of those arrangements aren't right or wrong. They're just different. And they can be changed at any time.

"As a matter of fact, your mother and I were just talking this week about allowances. You're getting older and very good about managing money. How does two dollars a week sound to start?"

I absolutely could not believe my ears! I didn't even have to ask! I know two dollars a week is not very much money and it's less than Jason gets for doing nothing, but as Dad said, it was a start.

I was on fire now! I was going to work even harder to get rid of the baby bunnies and pay off my debt. That night, I asked God to give me some ideas.

I woke up the next morning knowing exactly what to do. I was going to lower my price. Actually I would have given a rabbit away if anyone would take it. But I didn't want to put FREE on my sign. It would make it seem like the bunnies weren't worth anything. And I really did hope to earn some money.

I painted over my sign, "RABBITS $2.50."

Just as I was finishing, I heard the rumble of a logging truck coming down the road. The brakes squealed and the truck lurched to a stop in front of me.

"Excuse me there, miss," called the man behind the wheel. "Are you the one selling rabbits?"

I could hardly talk. Here was my first customer!

"Yes, I am," I finally managed to answer.

"Saturday is my boy's birthday. He'll be seven. Do you think that's old enough to take care of a rabbit?"

"I think so," I said. "They're not very hard to take care of. Come around back, and I'll show them to you."

The man was nice. We talked a long time about the rabbits and how to take care of

69

them. He told me all about his son.

"Do you live in Canada?" I asked, because most of the loggers did.

"Yes," he said, "but during the week, while we're working, we stay in a motel here in Maine."

"A motel?" I asked. "I thought loggers lived in a logging camp!"

"We do if we're working near one," he said.

"When you get back to your motel, be sure and show your friends this rabbit and tell them they're only two-fifty now. I've got seven left I want to sell."

The man said he would and drove away.

Later I laughed. My first customer was a logger, all right! But he wasn't crusty or old. He didn't even speak French! And my debt was down to two dollars and fifty cents.

70

For the next few days, I didn't think much about rabbits, because there was a certain traffic past my house that I couldn't ignore. Jason whizzed by on his Silver Streak every chance he got, calling out ramp progress reports at the top of his lungs.

"Hey, Tabitha! They moved the rosebushes last night!"

Great. I wished I could move.

"Hey, Tabitha! There's a front-end loader coming today to even out the bank. Come on down and watch!"

Right. I'd rather cut off my big toe.

"Hey, Tabitha! They're delivering the lumber today."

I went inside and delivered myself some orange juice.

"Gram, why does he have to rub it in? He's so mean. I wish he wouldn't ride it past our house."

"Don't worry," Grammy said. "That'll stop as soon as the ramp's built. When I

71

took her eggs down yesterday, Mrs. Harrington told me they had another kid in the emergency room with injuries from a skateboard accident. She's anxious to get that ramp done so Jason won't have to skate in the road."

I shoved Everett out of my way and slammed the refrigerator door. "I wish we could move."

"If we moved to another neighborhood," Grammy told me, "there would be someone else who irritates you, maybe even more than Jason does."

"No one could be worse than Jason."

"Stop it, Tabitha. You sit right here at this table until you can think of ten good things about Jason."

"Well, for one thing, he's not my brother!"

Grammy chuckled. "Go on."

"Uh, he's kind of cute, and he's good at science, and he's got neat curtains in his room. How many is that?"

Grammy frowned. "The curtains don't

count. That's three, and the first one is shaky."

"Uh . . . well, he doesn't swear as bad as most kids at school . . . he's kind to Hoppy and Everett and uh . . . once I heard Mr. Jepson say Jason was really good in Scouts. He's earned a ton of badges. Is that ten?"

"That's six."

"Oh, Grammy," I whined, "I can't

think of any more."

She wouldn't give up.

"Well," I said, "let's see. . . . he's not afraid of the dark, and . . . he's not afraid of bugs, and he's not afraid . . ."

" 'Not afraid' counts as one," Grammy interrupted. "Go on."

This was tough. "Well, once he helped me fix my bike, and . . . he doesn't call me Tabby anymore . . . and . . . he's got freckles."

"Well, there now," Grammy looked satisfied. "He doesn't sound like such an awful person after all, does he? I think we should invite him over for supper sometime."

I got out of there before Grammy decided to adopt him.

On Friday, a muddy pickup truck pulled into the driveway. I recognized the logging company's name on the side.

A man lifted a wooden crate out of the back.

74

"Did you come to look at the rabbits?" I asked.

"*Oui,*" he said. "Rabbit."

I took him around back to the chicken yard. When I opened the hutch, the man reached in and picked up Androcles.

"No," I said. "She's not for sale." I took her out of his arms and held her close to me.

"No?"

"No," I repeated. He may not have been very good with English, but he understood what I meant.

He reached back in and picked up one of the mostly white babies. "*Oui?*"

"Yes," I said. "*Oui.*" And the man plopped the bunny into his crate.

It was interesting to talk with someone without really talking. We understood each other just fine.

We went through the yes-and-no process until my customer had chosen four rabbits and closed them up in the crate.

75

He handed me a ten-dollar bill.

Oh, boy, is God answering prayer today!
I thought. I just kept staring at the money
while the man put the crate in the back of
the pickup and got in.

I gathered my wits and ran over to the
cab.

"Thank you," I said. "Thank you very
much."

He smiled and said, "Rabbit good *avec
des onions.*"

I smiled back at him. I didn't know what
he said, because I only knew about four
French words, but it sounded like aveck-
day-zawnyaw. I'd ask Grammy. Then I'd
know five French words.

But with my debt paid off and money left
over to add to my Silver Streak envelope, I
didn't think much about French. My worries
were over! Well, I still had Androcles and
Patricia and three extra bunnies, but my
pickle stew was almost gone . . . that is,
until that night at supper.

76

Daddy grinned, "Well, I hear my super salesgirl did all right today!"

I launched into the story of the French-Canadian logger who'd bought a whole crate load of rabbits and gotten me out of debt! I told them about how we could understand each other without really talking.

"He did know some English though. The last thing he said was 'Rabbit good,' and then he said something like 'aveck-day-zawnyaw.' "

Grammy dropped her fork. "What did he say?"

"Aveck-day-zawnyaw." I repeated it exactly as I had heard it.

"Oh." Grammy's face looked like she was trying to keep a secret.

I went back to eating my baked potato and chicken, but something about Grammy's weird reaction bothered me.

"Well, what does it mean, Grammy? What is 'aveck-day-zawnyaw.'"

Grammy kept looking back and forth from Mom to Daddy.

Daddy had his mouth full so he didn't say anything, but he sort of motioned with his fork to get Grammy going.

Grammy wiped her mouth with her napkin and said, "It means 'with onions.'"

·8·

Getting Hot

With onions? With onions! He was going to cook my rabbits!

Grammy got up and went into the kitchen.

I looked at Daddy, who was sputtering and wiping his mouth and the front of his shirt. Mom was staring at her plate. No one would look at me.

"Mom, that man is going to eat my rabbits! He's going to eat them!"

"Yes, it certainly sounds that way."

"We have to stop him! I'm going to call the lumber company and find that guy and get my rabbits back!" I shrieked. I stomped over to the phone and started flipping through the phone book.

Tears were getting in my eyes and I couldn't even see the pages. I slammed the book down and cried. Daddy put his arms around me.

"Tabitha, honey, it's probably already too late. This is Friday. The loggers go home to Canada for the weekend. Just let it go, sweetie."

"But, Daddy," I sobbed, "if I had known what he was going to do, I wouldn't have let him have them. I'd never eat a rabbit!"

"Honey, even if you would never eat a rabbit, lots of people do. It's quite an ordinary thing. The chicken you ate for supper was running around in the yard yesterday. Does that bother you?"

"No, it doesn't!" I shouted. "Chickens are stupid. They're supposed to be eaten! That's what they're for!"

"Well, it may surprise you, but rabbits are also 'supposed to be eaten.' They are one of the lowest things on the food chain.

80

All kinds of animals eat rabbits. If you hadn't rescued Androcles from the woods when you did, a coyote would have had her for dinner."

I went to bed early, but I couldn't sleep, of course. I kept thinking about my bunnies in a stewpot with onions!

I suppose I shouldn't blame the man. He was used to eating rabbits. And when he told me they were good with onions, what did I do? I smiled and nodded like I agreed with him.

The next morning, I took down my sign. There would be no more bunnies in the stewpot.

Then I went to my room and worked on some posters. "Free PET Rabbits." I made the word PET in big capital letters. I added my telephone number and a drawing of a large-red-and-white rabbit.

When Mom went shopping that afternoon, I went along. I tacked one sign on the bulletin board at the grocery store. I took one to the library, and several of the other store-keepers let me put one in their window.

Then we stopped at the veterinarian's, and Dr. Jonas hung a poster in his waiting room.

Mom knows the lady at the fabric store. "Sure I'll put one up," she said. "In fact, I'll hang it right here by the cash register. I'll point it out to people and tell them I know you."

On the way home, we stopped at Jason's house to watch the construction crew working on his ramp. It sloped down off the bank in back of the house, ran out across the "garden," and curled up sharply at the other end. The men were building the supports on the end that wasn't held up by the bank.

If this were in my backyard, Grammy would use those supports for pole beans and tomatoes. I'd be able to do a kick turn and have lunch all in one swift move.

Jason cruised up to our car window.

"Hi, Tabitha. Mom said you're not allowed to skate here without a helmet and pads. It's her rule."

"Don't worry, Jason. I can't skate here without a board."

"Well, you've got to get one then. Mom said I can have everybody over for a party after school starts."

I threw my mother a "please help" look, hoping she would change the subject. "Are you any good at this, Jason?" she asked.

That was the right thing to say. If you get Jason talking about himself, he forgets everything else.

"Watch this!" He whizzed down the driveway, did a swift little move over a broom handle, and then bowed to us expecting applause.

Mom and I went home.

All week long I jumped every time the phone rang. Finally one evening Dad answered it. "Yes, it is. Here I'll let you talk to my daughter. They're her rabbits."

The kid on the phone wanted a dwarf rabbit.

"Sorry," I told him. "I've never seen a dwarf rabbit. These rabbits are huge. I don't think they're what you want."

Then one day, I found a rabbit customer right in my own living room. She had come back for the last fitting of her wedding dress.

Just as I walked into the room, the lady said, "My little sister will miss me when I get married. We've shared a room ever since she was born and she'll be lonely."

I put forth my best effort in salesmanship. "Why don't you get her a pet?" I asked.

The lady turned in a rustle of white and looked at me in surprise. "That's a good idea! Maybe I will."

"She would probably like a rabbit," I said. "I have three pretty ones for free. The vet says they can be trained to use a litter

84

box just like a cat."

The lady started to laugh. "That would really be something. My name is Bonnie, but she has always called me Bunny. I'll get her a bunny to replace me when I leave!"

Bunny, who wanted a bunny, turned out to be a problem. The rabbit she wanted was Patricia.

"Look," she said at last, "that really is

the only one I like. You don't have to give her to me. I'll pay you five dollars for her and I'll keep her name Patricia. I'll even tell my sister that if she ever has to find a new home for her, to give her back to you. How about it?"

I weighed the advantages of keeping the rabbit and feeding her, against the advantages of having another five dollars toward my skateboard. I voted for the Silver Streak.

•9•

Boiling Over

All things considered, I had handled my pickle stew pretty well up to that point. I was rid of most of the babies, and I was out of debt. I was getting an allowance and had money saved toward my Silver Streak. I didn't miss Patricia, and I only thought about rabbit stew every now and then.

And I had done all of this without Jason's help. I didn't see much of him now that his ramp was done.

Two weeks before school started, Mom and Dad had an anniversary. They went out to eat at the Chinese restaurant with a gift certificate Grammy had given them.

Daddy looked so handsome in his

black sweater, and I had always thought Mom was pretty, but that night she looked fantastic.

"Fifteen years," Mom said. "Richard, I just can't believe we've been married that long!"

"Well, I could stand another fifteen years surrounded by beautiful women," Daddy said, glancing at me out of the corner of his eye.

I threw a pillow at him, but he snatched it out of the air and threw it back before I could even blink. I can never catch him off guard.

I went outside with them to say good-bye, and I noticed that all the chickens were inside the coop. Every one of them! I hurried to shut their door. I'd come out later and put Androcles in her hutch. She and her three babies were still sleeping in a pile under the maple tree.

In the kitchen Grammy was making macaroni and cheese, but the dog was under the table instead of pacing back and

88

forth under her feet.

I leaned down to talk to him. "Hey, Everett, you're neglecting your dogly duty. Whenever someone's cooking, you're supposed to try and trip them, remember?" Everett whined and scooted back closer to the wall.

"Is Jason here yet?" Grammy asked. I glanced out the window toward his house. "No, I don't see him coming. Gram, do you really think this is a good idea? Jason and I can't keep from arguing for five minutes. It'll spoil my appetite."

"Tabitha, don't worry about Jason. If you are friendly and agreeable, he won't have anyone to argue with. Just try being a good hostess. Now, why don't we eat here in the kitchen tonight?"

By the time I got the table set, Jason had appeared at the back door. "There's a storm coming," he announced. "It's getting windy and the sky's black over there behind the hill."

89

"So that's why the chickens went in early," I said. "Maybe they're smarter than I thought."

"They're not smart," Jason said. "They're just chicken."

I groaned at his joke and pointed to Everett under the table. "Look who else is chicken. If the storm gets really loud, he'll be practically in our laps."

"The chickens may be smart, but we're not," Grammy said. "We've got every window in the house open."

We made a mad dash to close the windows just as the storm broke overhead, crashing and whipping around the house. As we ate, Everett whined and pushed against our legs with every clap of thunder, while the wind and rain beat against the windows. Then a great cracking rip sounded above the noise of the storm.

"There goes another branch of the maple tree," Grammy said. "Sounds like a big one this time."

"Boy, I'm sure glad I'm not outside in . . ." I stopped in the middle of my sentence as a horrible thought struck me. Androcles!

I jumped up from the table so fast that I sent Everett sprawling. "Gram, the rabbits are still out! They were sleeping under the tree!"

I was out the door in a flash. The tree had split and fallen against the gate. I couldn't see the rabbits, and I couldn't get past the broken tree into the chicken yard.

"Tabitha! Put this on. You'll be soaked to the skin."

I turned around to see Grammy leaning over the railing, holding out my raincoat. Thunder exploded again right overhead. Grammy jumped at the sound and clutched the handrail for support. But it didn't hold her. She cried out as the railing pulled away from the steps, and I saw her crumple in a heap on the ground.

I couldn't have been more than ten steps away, but it seemed to take me forever to get to her. "Grammy, are you okay?" She didn't answer. It looked like she was dead.

I screamed and screamed and that was all I could do. I just stood there and screamed, until I realized that someone was shaking me hard.

"Tabitha," Jason was saying, "go get Mr. Jepson. He'll call the ambulance."

I started to sob, but Jason gave me a shove and shouted, "Run!"

So I ran. When Mr. Jepson and I got back to Grammy, Jason had covered her with the coats that had been hanging on the back porch. He was holding up my raincoat like a tent to keep the wind and water out of her face.

There, holding down the other end of the "tent," was Everett, lying close to Grammy with the raincoat pinned between them.

Grammy looked up at me and tried to smile.

"Why didn't you answer me, Grammy? I thought you were dead! Can't you get up?"

92

"She's not bleeding anywhere," Jason shouted over the noise of the storm. "But I think she's broken something. She's in a lot of pain."

Thunder rumbled overhead, and Grammy's voice was weak and shaky. "Is the ambulance coming?"

"We called them," Mr. Jepson said. He bent down and touched her face. "They said to keep you warm and not to move you until they got here."

Jason handed me the end of the raincoat. "Here, hold this. I'll try to find something better."

He came out in a minute with some blankets and a sofa pillow and the big white plastic tablecloth off the dining room table.

The tablecloth made a much better tent. It covered all of her, and we took off the wet coats and tucked the warm, dry blankets around her. We couldn't do anything about Everett, though. He wouldn't budge.

93

"Jason, how did you make him come outside in this storm?" I hollered as lightning flashed and the dog snuggled closer to Grammy.

Jason shrugged. "I didn't make him do anything. When she fell, he practically knocked me over getting out the door."

Good old Everett.

The ambulance was taking forever. Grammy was groaning and crying a little, but the storm was dying down.

Mr. Jepson put the raincoat around my shoulders and handed his umbrella to Jason. "What's the name of the restaurant where your folks went, Tabitha?"

"It's that Chinese place. I think they left the number by the telephone."

He went inside to call Mom and Dad, and I ran to the road to look for the ambulance.

It was only just raining now, and the wind wasn't so bad, but I felt so sorry for Grammy lying there in pain on the wet ground.

At last I heard the siren in the distance and ran back to tell the others.

Mr. Jepson was just coming down the steps. "I got your parents," he said. "They'll meet us at the hospital. I'll ride along in the ambulance, and your mom said you are to go to Jason's. They'll call you there as soon as she's settled. Now, run back out to the road and wave, so they can see which house it is."

A little while later Grammy was bundled into the back of the ambulance. I stood in the rain at the edge of the road, watching them take her away, and burst into tears.

Jason's voice behind me made me jump. "Come on. Let's go. I called my mom. She said to put Everett inside and bring dry clothes."

"I can't go yet," I sobbed. "This all happened because I left my rabbits out. I don't know where they are, and the tree is lying on the gate. It's probably killed them. I've got to find them before it gets dark."

Jason climbed over the fence and tugged

95

at the tree. "I can't move it, Tabitha. You'll have to climb over."

But I didn't. I sat down in the mud in the middle of the driveway and cried. My rabbits were gone and my Grammy was gone and it was all my fault.

Jason called to me from under the broken tree. "I don't see them anywhere, Tabitha. They're not here."

96

He scrambled out from under the wet branches, shaking himself like a dog. Then he went over to the rabbit hutch and peered inside. He shut the door and turned around.

"Stop crying, Tabitha." Jason sounded disgusted. "Your dumb rabbits are more worried about missing their supper than they are about the storm. They're all in the hutch lined up at the feed tray, waiting for you to feed them."

97

Leftovers

I wasn't allowed to see Grammy at first. Then when Mom finally took me to the hospital, Grammy wasn't even in her room. A nurse told us she was downstairs in X ray. We sat down to wait.

At last a man in a green jumpsuit brought Grammy in a wheelchair. With her leg in a cast and propped straight out in front of her, she looked small and very pale.

I burst into tears, and Grammy took my hand and patted it, like she does when I have a fever.

"Tabitha, don't worry so much. I'm going to be fine. I only have to stay here a few more days."

"Grammy," I sobbed, "it's all because of me and my dumb rabbits. If it weren't for me, you wouldn't have gotten hurt. You probably hate me for that."

Mom suddenly decided she needed some coffee. "I'll bring you a cup of tea," she said to Gram, and took off to find the snack bar.

Grammy made me stop crying and look at her. Then she said something really unbelievable.

"Tabitha, did you push me off the porch steps?"

At first I didn't think I had heard her right. "Gram . . . how can you think? . . ."

"Well then, were you glad when I fell?"

At that my tears started gushing all over again.

"Grammy, of course not! I love you!"

"Of course you do. And I love you. So how in the world can you think this was your fault? I knew that railing was bad. It was just an accident, plain and simple."

"But if I hadn't left my rabbits out,

99

none of this would have happened."

"Maybe not, but let's not hear any more talk like that. Trouble happens no matter how we try to avoid it. You of all people should know that."

Grammy shifted in her chair a little and smoothed her bathrobe down. "How are your rabbits anyway? Your dad told me they weren't hurt by the storm."

"They're okay. Daddy gave one away yesterday to a guy who works at the dairy, and the lady at the fabric store took one for her nephew."

"Great! That means only one to go, right?"

I nodded. "I got some more phone calls from my posters. Someone's coming this evening to look at the last bunny."

Grammy smiled and clapped her hands. "Then that's the end of your pickle stew. But you don't look very happy. Are you having trouble with Jason again?"

"No, he's all right." I went to the door

and looked down the hall to see if Mom were coming yet. "Gram, do you think Jason would still hang around with me if there were any boys on our road?"

"Oh, he might. Why do you ask?"

"Well, you know that night you came to the hospital, and I went to his house? While I was in the bathroom, I heard him telling his mother that my crying made him very nervous. He said, 'I knew just what to do for her grandmother, but I sure didn't know what to do for her.'

"And his mom said, 'It's always harder to think straight when someone you really care for is upset.'

"Then do you know what he said? He said, 'Yeah, I guess she is practically my best friend, even if she is a girl.' "

Grammy's eyes were wide. "No kidding?"

We didn't say anything for a long time. I sat and fiddled with the zipper on the pocket of my jeans.

Finally I broke the silence. "Grammy, I thought all my rabbit trouble was terrible. But now look what's happened to you. The pickle stew I had was nothing compared to this."

"Tabitha, the doctor is very pleased with how I'm healing. Sixty is not really old, you know. I think all the vitamins and calcium your mom makes me take must have helped."

I stretched and rubbed my shoulder. "Well, I'm going to take a while to heal. After the storm, Daddy cut down the rest of the maple tree. He chopped up all the wood and sold it to Mr. Jepson. Guess who got to wheel it across the road and stack it?"

I raised my hand and waved it in the air. "Tabitha Sarah Bigbee, that's who. I must have made at least eighty thousand trips with that wagon."

Grammy chuckled. "Well, you sure have a lot of experience hauling wood. Maybe your daddy was right. You'd make a great lumberjack."

"Oh, Grammy!"

"Honey, we might as well make light of it. All our lives we get out of one stew and right into the next. It's because of sin in the world."

"I try not to sin, Grammy."

"That's not what I mean. Oh, we can get into trouble on purpose, and we all do. But we also have lots of trouble and pain that's not our fault. That's pickle stew, and everyone in the whole world has got it."

I folded my arms across my chest and slid way down in my chair. "It's not fair."

"No, it's not, but it won't last forever. Remember last year, when you asked Jesus to take away the sin in your heart?"

"Yeah. You told me Jesus is the only one who could fix things up between God and me."

"Right. The sin in your heart separated you from God. The sin in the world separates the whole world from God. But someday when Jesus comes back to earth He's going to fix everything.

"Then, there won't be too many rabbits. There will be just enough, and loggers won't eat them. There won't be thunderstorms that split trees. Porch railings won't break, and neither will old ladies' legs."

I could get into this.

104

"And neighbor boys won't be rude?"

Grammy nodded. "Moms and dads won't worry about bills, and firewood won't need to be stacked. In the meantime, God helps us work out ways to handle the pickle stew."

Mom appeared in the doorway, holding a piece of paper. "I never made it to the snack bar," she said, "but I did run into Gerta Sorensen. She gave me this."

I took the paper Mom held out to me and read it aloud:

Northern Maine Rabbit Breeders
Fall Show
Sanctioned Competition and
General Exhibition
All Breeds

Mom pointed to all the small print at the bottom. "See, it says here they're starting a junior division for exhibitors twelve and under. Gerta said she'd help you get your rabbit ready to show. They're aren't many red satins in this area, and she'd like you to enter Androcles."

"Maybe," I said, "maybe I will."

A nurse came with Grammy's supper.

"We're going to have to get started home," Mom said to me. "We have a stop to make along the way, and maybe we'll pick up a pizza for supper."

Then she turned to Grammy. "You get better and come home soon. Richard won't say it to my face, but I think he misses your cooking."

"Everett misses you too, Gram," I said. "Mom doesn't drop little pieces of food on the floor for him when she cooks."

Gram laughed right out loud. "You tell Everett anything I drop is purely accidental. I'm getting old, remember?"

On the way home in the car, Mom reached into her pocket and handed me an envelope.

On the outside, it said:

To my junior lumberjack,
This is for pulling your weight,
and for pulling the weight of an entire
maple tree.
                    Love, Dad.

Inside were two twenty-dollar bills.

"Mom, look at all this money. Dad paid me!"

"Well, Mr. Jepson paid him for the wood. Dad said you did half the work, so you should get half the money. Now, do you think we have time to stop at the mall? I have a feeling there's something at SportCity you'd like to spend your money on."

"Mom, what if the price has gone up? My other money's at home in my night-stand."

Mom only smiled and handed me another envelope. It had NOT FOR RABBITS scribbled on the outside. "I thought you might want it," she said.

She laughed as she turned the car into the mall parking lot. "Are you sure there's nothing you need here?"

"Well, come to think of it," I said, as though I were trying to decide, "I think there might be something I need to buy at SportCity . . ." I crammed the money deep into my jeans pocket and zipped it shut, ". . . especially if it has a silver streak."